JULIE RHODES is a professional wildlife artist who lives in Cornwall with her husband and baby daughter. Their boxer dog Archie inspired Julie to write *The Very Noisy House*. Julie says, "Archie is always barking and running about, so our house is very noisy!" She has written and illustrated stories for her family all her life, but this is her first published book.

KORKY PAUL was born in Zimbabwe and is one of seven children. He studied Fine Art at Durban Art School in South Africa and Film Animation at CalArts in California. Known only to himself as the 'World's Greatest Portrait Painter and Dinosaur Drawer', Korky regularly holds drawing workshops at libraries and schools to encourage children to share his passion for drawing. He is also the illustrator of the picture book *Snail's Legs* by Damian Harvey. He lives with his family in Oxford.

For Amelia with all my love – JR

To Colleen Forder for getting me my first job – KP

A big thank you to Church Cowley St James C of E Primary School,
Oxford for helping with the endpapers – KP
Front endpapers by Kara Parsons age 9 and Ragul Sivakurunathan age 9
Back endpapers by Waqas Memood age 11 and Amelia Westlake age 10

First published in Great Britain in 2013 and in the USA in 2014 by
Frances Lincoln Children's Books, 74-77 White Lion Street,
London N1 9PF
www.franceslincoln.com

First paperback edition published in 2013

A CIP catalogue record for this book is available from the British Library

ISBN 978-1-8478-0534-8

Illustrated with watercolours

Set in Russisch Brot LT

Printed in China

THE VERY NOISY HOUSE

Written by Julie Rhodes
Illustrated by Korky Paul

F

FRANCES LINCOLN

CHILDREN'S BOOKS

At the bottom of the very tall house lived an old lady.

She walked with the help of a BIG wooden stick.

"CLOMP, CLOMP, CLOMP," went the stick as she crossed the room.

"CLOMP, CLOMP, CLOMP."

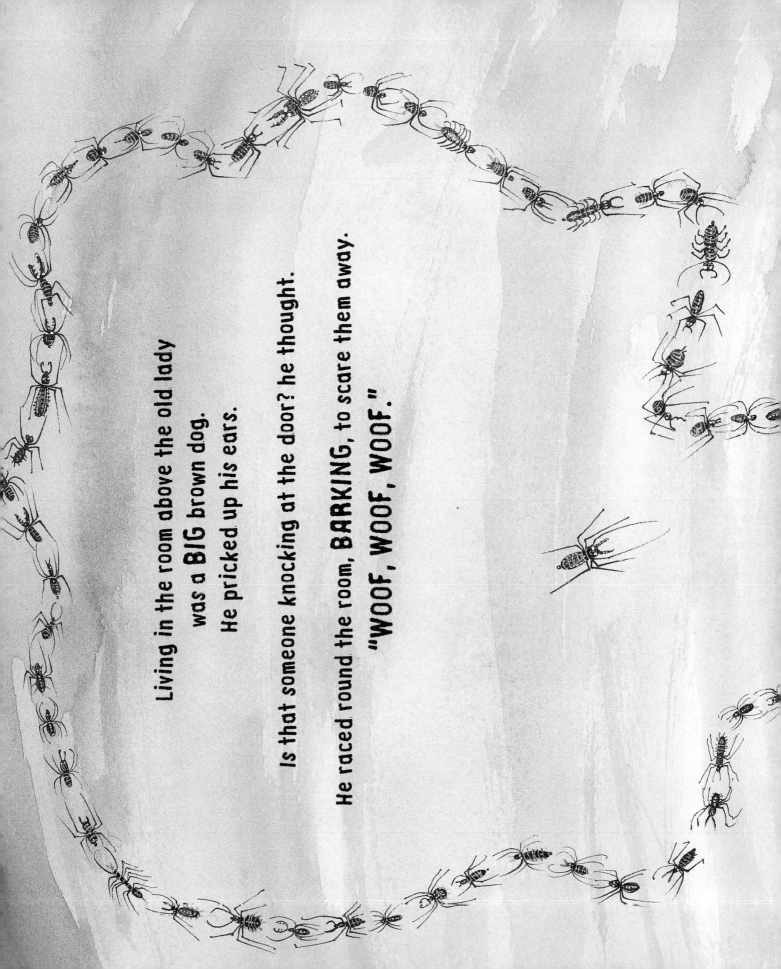

Living in the room above the old lady
was a **BIG** brown dog.
He pricked up his ears.

Is that someone knocking at the door? he thought.

He raced round the room, **BARKING**, to scare them away.
"WOOF, WOOF, WOOF."

In the room above the dog,
a small ginger cat was quietly sleeping.

She opened one eye.

Is that a dog barking? It must be after me, she thought.

She began to meow LOUDLY with fright.
"MEOW, MEOW, MEOW."

CLOMP! CLOMP! CLOMP!

In the room above the ginger cat,
a baby was PLAYING in his cot.
He heard the frightened cat MEOWING
and the noise upset him.

A tear rolled down his cheek and he began to cry.
"WHAAA, WHAAA, WHAAA."

In the attic above the baby were five roosting birds and they were disturbed by the noisy baby crying.

They FLUTTERED, squawking, into the air.
"SQUAWK, SQUAWK, SQUAWK."

SQUAWK!SQUAWK!SQUAWK!

SQUAWK!SQUAWK!SQUAWK!

SQUAWK!SQUAWK!SQUAWK!SQUAWK!

WHAAA!WHAAA!WHAAA!

MEOW!MEOW!MEOW!

MEOW!MEOW!MEOW!

MEOW!MEOW!MEOW!

e baby heard the squawking birds
d didn't like the sound.

cried even HARDER.

WHAAA!WHAAA!WHAAA!

EOW!MEOW!MEOW!

e ginger cat listened.
the baby crying
d was frightened
the sound.

e MEOWED even more.

MEOW!MEOW!MEOW!

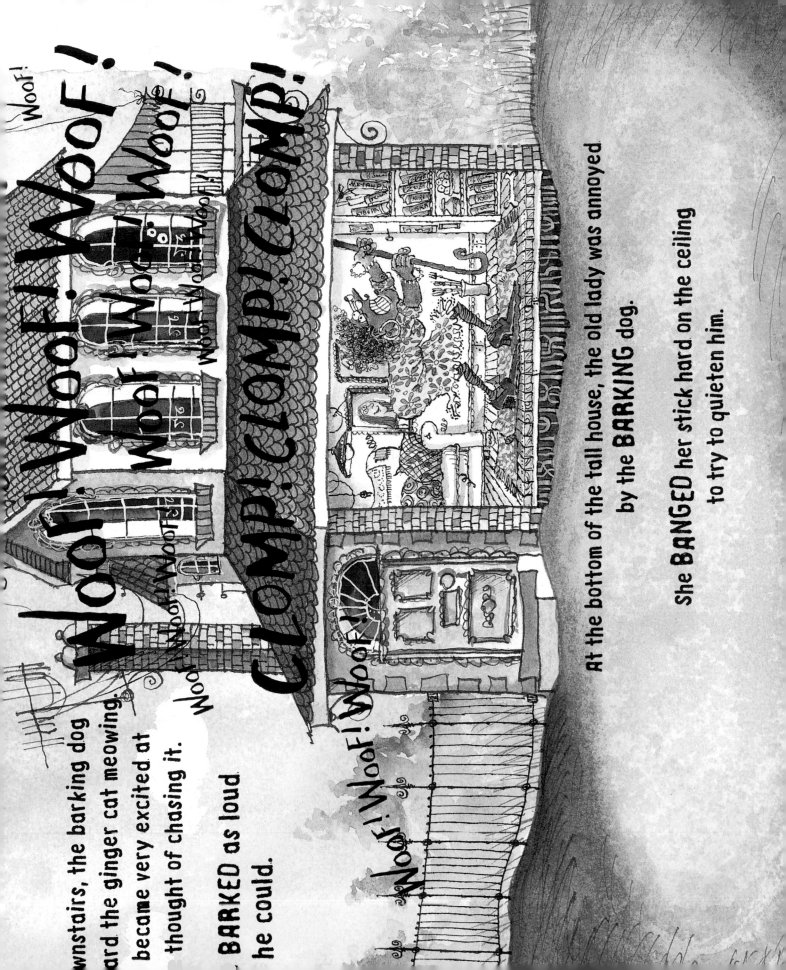

Woof!

Woof! Woof! Woof! Woof! Woof! Woof! Woof! Woof! Woof! Woof! Woof! Woof! Woof! Woof! Woof!

CLOMP! CLOMP! CLOMP!

Woof! Woof! Woof!

...wnstairs, the barking dog
...ard the ginger cat meowing.
...became very excited at
...thought of chasing it.

...BARKED as loud
...he could.

Woof! Woof! Woof!

At the bottom of the tall house, the old lady was annoyed
by the BARKING dog.

She BANGED her stick hard on the ceiling
to try to quieten him.

Meow!! Meow!!
Woof! Woof! Woof! Woof! Woof!
Woof! Woof! Woof! Woof! Woof! Woof!
Woof! Woof! Woof! Woof! Woof! Woof!
Woof! Woof! Woof! Woof! Woof! Woof!
Woof! Woof! Woof!

CLICK, CLICK, CLICKETY-CLICK

At the sound of the banging, the dog BARKED louder than ever. The old lady decided to sit in her favourite chair and do some knitting to take her mind off the noise.

"CLICK, CLICK, CLICKETY-CLICK," went the knitting needles.

CLICK, CLICK, CLICKETY CLICK

The brown dog listened to the RHYTHM of the clicking needles and began to feel SLEEPY. He stopped barking and settled down in his basket.

CLICK, CLICK, CLICKETY CLICK

The cat could no longer hear the barking
so she closed her eyes and went quietly to sleep.

CLICK, CLICK, CLICK, CLICKETY CLICK

The baby was soothed by the sound of silence and drifted off to sleep.

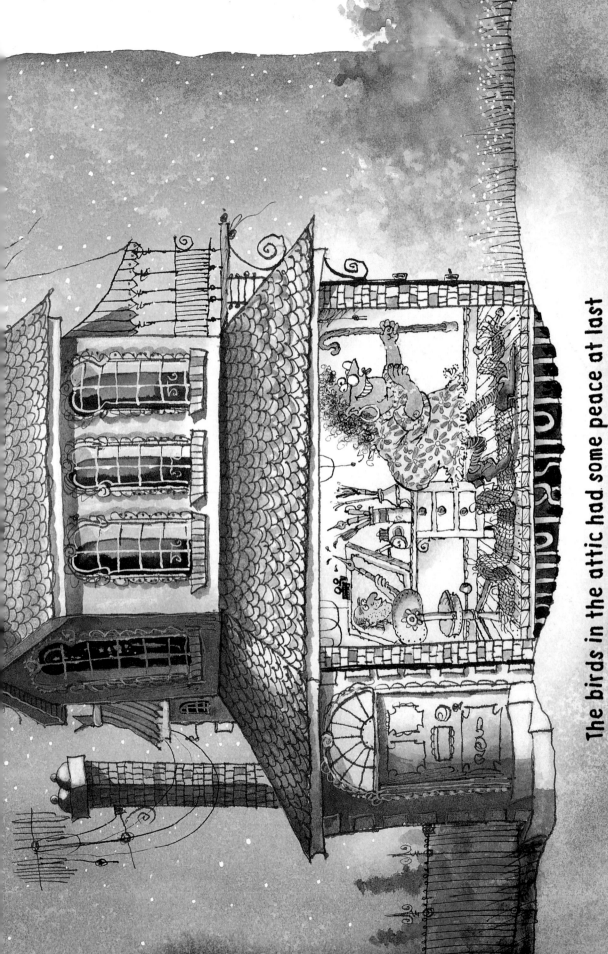

The birds in the attic had some peace at last
and fluttered quietly down to roost.

"Ahh," said the old lady. "I shall make a nice cup of tea."
She got up from her chair and picked up her walking stick.

CLOMP! CLOMP! CLOMP!

"CLOMP, CLOMP, CLOMP," went the stick as she crossed the room.

"CLOMP, CLOMP, CLOMP."

The BIG, brown dog pricked up his ears....

ALSO ILLUSTRATED BY KORKY PAUL
FOR FRANCES LINCOLN CHILDREN'S BOOKS...

SNAIL'S LEGS
Damian Harvey

Snail and Frog are the fastest runners in the whole wood.
When a chef arrives in search of the strongest legs to help
him prepare a special birthday treat for the King, the two
friends argue over who will have the great honour. So they
decide to settle the matter with a race. Frog is determined
to beat Snail. But what reward will the King bestow on
the strongest legs in the kingdom?

"Brilliantly detailed comic illustrations." – *The School Librarian*